Preparing A Place

[for myself]

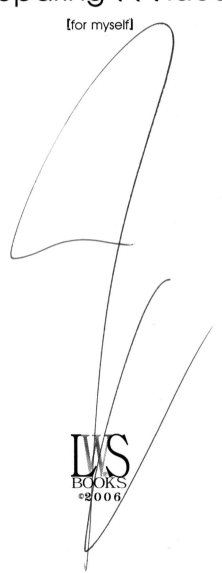

LWS
BOOKS
©2006

Also from Jonathan Richard Cring

FICTION:
I'M . . . the legend of the son of man
Liary
Mr. Kringle's Tales . . . 26 stories 'til Christmas
Holy Peace

NONFICTION:
Jesonian
Finding the Lily (to consider)
Digging for Gold (in the rule)
Preparing a Place (for myself)

SCREENPLAYS:
Hank's Place
Lenders Morgan
The Man with the Red Hat (short)
Baptism 666
Gobel
Iz and Pal
Newer
Inside (short)

MUSICAL COMPOSITIONS:
I'M . . . a Jesonian serenade
Cloud of Witnesses (a requiem of renewal)
Have yourself a Clazzy Little Christmas
To Everything a Season – Ingathering/Crystalline
To Everything a Season – Primavera/Soulstace
Opus 9/11
Symprophecy 2003
Jack
Symprophecy 2004
Being Human Symphony Live
Another Lily for You
Clazzy O - Let

2

Preparing a Place

[for Myself]

Jonathan Richard Cring

LWS Books
P.O. Box 833
Hendersonville, TN 37077-0833
(800) 643-4718 ext. 74
lwsbooks.com

LWS Books are available at special quantity discounts for
bulk purchases for sales promotions, premiums, fund-
raising, and educational needs. Special books or book
excerpts also can be created to fit specific needs.
For details, write: LWS Books Special Markets,
P.O. Box 833, Hendersonville, TN 37077

ISBN 978-0-9704361-6-0

Library of Congress Control Number: 2005907938

For information on the authors touring schedule visit:
WWW.JANETHAN.COM

Cover Design by Angela Cring, Clazzy Studios

Manufactured and Printed in the United States

Here we go . . .

Sitting One

I died today.

I didn't expect it to happen. Then again, I did—well, not really.

A shock.

I wasn't actually sick suddenly. I suppose if I went back and analyzed the downgrade, I would uncover a hundred little symptoms; great clues to my demise. Still, some mystery.

I'm not an expert on the subject of dying, but it really seems easier if you don't fight it. Gasping and struggling just prolong the aggravation.

No, I certainly didn't expect it.

Death is like an appointment with a tailor to have your tux altered. You know you will eventually need to go and do it, but still not in a particular hurry to have someone measure, chalk, and estimate your width and breadth. No—no one is really in a hurry to be fitted, tux or casket.

Another thought, wow.

I've had moments of clarity in my life. Amazingly enough, many of them were in the midst of a dream. For a brief second, I would know the meaning of life or the missing treatment to cure cancer. And then as quickly as it popped into my mind it was gone.

The same thing just happened. It's interesting. I don't remember much about my last breath. I really don't recollect dying. Just this unbelievable sense of clear-headedness, like walking into a room newly painted and knowing by the odor and brightness that the color on the wall is so splattering new that you should be careful not to touch it for fear of smearing the design.

It's a rush.

A typhoon of knowledge.

A freshness in the mind, like chilled air smacking your face on a frosty morn; pure oxygen instead of smothering smog. Suddenly, things make sense. Ideas are crowding to get in.

So now, I guess, with the lack of attention to a body, and the fear of death disclosed as a myth, wisdom has a chance, maybe for the first time in a long time, to enlighten. It sounds ethereal, but no. There is nothing particularly heavenly about it, nor is it some great unveiling from the Ultimate Ethos.

It's just there—suddenly mine.

The greatest revelation of all?

I don't know why I didn't see it when I was alive and human—wait, yes I do. Because everything I believed in was based upon this "thing." Each action was dependent upon it, and all progress I earned subject to its power and will.

Here it is.

The first astounding realization upon crossing to the other side is that there is no other world; merely the jubilation of discovering that time really does not exist.

Time was God's creation to cause the earth to have some regularity—a cycle—a measure of stability.

But twenty-five miles in the sky time ceases to exist.

The planet Pluto takes two hundred forty-eight years to circle the sun. It doesn't give a damn.

The universe is not nearly as vast as it is present.

The day of my death was the day I became free of the only burden I really ever had. I never considered it to be cumbersome, but now it looms as the most hideous ogre in my brief history as an inhabitant of Planet Earth: TIME.

Useless.

Time is fussy. Time is worry.

Time is fear. Time is the culprit causing human-types to recoil from pending generosity.

There just was never enough time.

Time would not allow it.

Remember—"if time permits?"

Why if time permits? Why not if *I* permit? Why not if *I* dream? Why not if *I* want? Why does time get to dictate to me my passage?

It was amazing. As the burst of revelation swept my soul and my mind opened, I realized the old hymn that stated, "When we've been there ten thousand years" has an unfortunate wording. I do recall sitting in church, listening to that hymn and thinking to myself, "My God, I get fidgety watching television for three hours. How can I be in Heaven for ten thousand years?" Even absolute bliss and serenity would become a gnawing boredom in such a span. And then, on top of that, to consider spending ten thousand years singing and praising caused me to wish that somewhere along the line there would be a peaceful end to it all.

It never occurred to me that the created adversary of mankind—time— would be slaughtered at death.

Yes, time, executed by the great eternal wisdom of the universe, is replaced with the careful vigil of spirit. Yes, that's it. As I entered the aftermath of my human completion, I accepted that spirit is merely the absence of time. Say it again—SPIRIT IS THE ABSENCE OF TIME.

It was time that robbed me of my soulful nature. It was time that caused me to be a sniveling carnal mass of nervous energy. It was time that convinced me that my selfishness was needed. It was time that allowed me to wheedle and deedle my way out of true emotion.

I didn't die.

The clock in me died, leaving spirit to tick on.

In one of my newly anointed moments of perception, I thought of the words, "God is spirit." I used to try and wrap my mind around the concepts of omnipresence and omniscience. How could God be everywhere at the same time? How could God be all knowing?

Because God is spirit, and spirit cannot exist in the same structure with time. God, being spirit, had no time. Time, being gone, left no restrictions. Not restricted—everything is reachable—all things possible.

So what was the purpose for time in the original scheme?

Time was the harsh reminder that we were cocooned in a temporary, human process of metamorphosis; hibernation, if you will, perhaps an experiment—no, hibernation is much better. Therefore, we needed some sort of pacing to eek away the moments until we could be translated to fly away from the constraints of seconds, minutes, hours, days, weeks, months, years, decades, and—I almost said—centuries. Isn't it amazing that really very few mortals are granted one century of breathing earth-life existence? We all begin and end in the unimpressive passage of less than one hundred years— usually much less.

So why don't we see the farce of time? Why do we allow ourselves to fall under the power of the cruel despot? Yes, time is a relentless master—very little wage for much demand.

I died today.

Actually, a piece of time named after me was cast away.

It is finished.

Sitting Two

I giggled. When I was in flesh, if I had laughed this hard, I would have needed to catch my breath, my heart racing. Not now. My laughter soars—it echoes, it rings, it expands, and it is without need of air or apology. It is wild, unabandoned and unashamed.

I laughed some more.

Another thought. More words.

"No time like the present."

How could I have been so stupid? There *is* no time—just the present. Everything else is either fictitious or sentimental. The past always desired to draw my soul into yearning or shame. The future aggravated me with its uncertainty and teased me with its promise.

Damn them both.

And a special damning, if you don't mind, for time that spawned those two infidels—past and future.

There is no time, just the present.

Relieved of time, I am able to flow. Brief thoughts pepper my mind. Where is God? Where is the tunnel to heaven?

God is a spirit. I am a spirit. I was created in his image. Now no longer merely a creation, the vessel broken open,

I have become part of the spirit of God. Heaven is not a place. If it were a place, there would be need for a journey, and therefore the need for time and time doesn't exist. Heaven is to be with God, and God is a spirit. And to be with a spirit, you must be spirited. To be spirited is to abandon the chains of time.

Time does not exist. (Oh, I said that already.)

Now, replacing the daily drudgery is the explosion of experience—surrounded by everything, all at once, yet, simultaneously, I can indwell the inner thoughts of a single ant without even a breath of distinction between the two visitations.

If I feel the desire to be there, I am there.

I am everywhere. Once everywhere, I was back again, to desire again, to begin again, although it never really began and certainly never ended, because time did not pass.

This shouldn't boggle my mind. We all had a precursor to this experience—sleep. Sleep had been a passage, a door where we were permitted to pass between the world of time and the universe of spirit.

Think about it. When we sleep, there is no sense of time. One minute, one hour—makes no difference. Our dreams are not metered. They flow quickly or slowly, based on the unction of spirit rather than the constraints of Mr. Tick-Tock. What I never realized—oh, my dear God, how could I realize it?—was that the earthly existence continues to evolve, that without this evolution, the world would destroy itself. So often, quietly, while sleeping, sweet and gentle realizations and transitions may occur, where we awaken to a new and different world, having no consciousness of its changing because of the subtleties of a wise and prudent God who makes adjustments without interfering too much in the general welfare.

Do you understand what I am saying? Of course not. You didn't die today. I did.

It just means that while we sought for miracles, using our planet-bound senses of eyes and ears and nose, that God simply and quietly did miracles in the only realm where miracles are permitted—the realm of spirit, free of the bondage of time. So while we slept, the pain that wracked our bodies the night before, that we thought was the ache of weariness, was healed in the night, some sort of tumor that would have caused our death.

It is in the realm of sleep where our spirit is allowed to enter the presence of God for fine-tuning and fellowship.

The idea is expansive. We may go to sleep the father of two sons, to awaken to a family of three boys and one girl, never sensing the difference, never knowing the addition—God, in his wisdom, granting us a blessing without us having to consciously struggle with the transformation.

It is a process called *mortalation*.

For somewhere, there is always a child who needs a home. Somewhere there is always a sickness that needs healing. And somewhere there is always a dream that needs to be awakened.

Sleep. The simulation of death. The escape from time. The entrance to the world of spirit. How ironic it is that each of us yearns for sleep, craves even the smallest nap, where we escape, no longer bound by our mortal bodies, floating in the realm of spiritual awareness and ecstasy; yet at the same time, we fear death, the ultimate journey of sleep into the adventure of spiritual completeness.

I'm sorry, I had to laugh again. Did I tell you how wonderful it is not to be breathless? Wait. I guess I am completely breathless.

But unafraid.

Sitting Three

I made a few visits.

For instance, cockroaches think of humans as really large road construction.

Flies like the feel of our skin.

Cats find us needy.

Dogs think we are part of their pack.

Snakes are very, very scared of us.

A brook does not worry, but it does try very hard to stay together.

Lions are susceptible to depression. Centipedes love to run.

Caterpillars are self-conscious of their furriness.

It goes on and on. How wonderful to be spirit, to just go in and out of all the creatures of the planet—of the universe.

Did I mention there are two universes? I think I forgot to say that. There is a new heaven and a new earth. While traversing through one I was abruptly extolling the virtues of the second.

When I was human (which, by the way, I still feel very human), I was always intrigued about heaven. All the religions of the world speculate on the afterlife. Facts are, Eternity is morsels of all and bigger than each.

Point: We do not come back as cows. But I can tell you that a cow is very proud of its milk. We certainly don't walk on streets of gold, but in this present moment, I am visiting a planet that is solid gold and feels absolutely no opulence about it whatsoever. And there is something beyond the grave, yet if it is the grave you desire, a sense of nothingness, then it is the grave you shall have. For you see, it was the Nazarene who said he would go to prepare a place for us. Why do we forget that? Let me tell you, Heaven is not a place where we clump together like dust bunnies, trying to submit to a common cause. Eternity is spirit, where each may pursue the heart's desire that during the mortal journey was restricted by time, shame and responsibility.

Time, shame and responsibility. The trio of demons tormenting all humanity, each acting as benevolent benefactor when really a cruel jailor.

Time—the meticulous conglomeration of moments to the exclusion of spirit.

Shame—the agonizing recounting of failed vision.

Responsibility—the aching drip of water, nagging us continually of our duty and inadequacy.

I curse you three demons, and I revel in a spirit that allows me to be free of your dreadful repose.

A place for us. Yes. I just remembered the song: *There's a place for us, somewhere a place for us.*

Somewhere over the rainbow—believe you me, way over the rainbow.

How remarkable. Even in our mortal, mental prisons, we had flashes of revelation of what would come.

To dream the impossible dream.

Listen to the words of our poets. For it is often the poet who inspires the prophet. It is the poet who grows weary of time long before the laborer. It is the poet that dreams of a place where restrictions are lifted and passion is no longer censored.

No wonder God referred to breath as spirit.

Everything, in this present state, is like a breath. No, even lighter than that. Earth was so laden and heavy, burdened with the weight of fear—movement exhausting.

Now all is lighter than breath.

No longer pursuit, just acquisition.

Not dream, relinquishment. Oh, what an absolutely blessed word—relinquish.

I just found out that flowers turn their faces toward the sun to gain energy. Astounding.

Sitting Four

I just emerged from the most incredible concert. It was a concert of my music, played by the Eternals. Arrangements that existed in my mind as only passing fancies or mulled over notions, exploded in sound before me. Symphonies I had written, fantasizing the inclusion of a thousand violins and a hundred basses were far surpassed by the magnificent aura of music cascading over my soul.

My music. Performed by excited gregarians of sound and talent. Music coming from everywhere—thundering, filling the heavens with the melodies I conceived when mortal and that I prayed would be immortalized long after my human journey.

A realization. I was hearing the combined orchestras of the entire universe! They had been granted the score of my pen to play on their instruments—tinklings, tappings, tenors and timbrels—beyond imagination—threatening near-creative lunacy.

Then there were voices resounding across the cosmos, speaking words, jumbled at first and muddled, gradually bursting with the purity of a thousand cornets. They were my words. Sentiments of this fledgling, novice spirit-man now echoed throughout all creation. Phrases from my books; thoughts from my heart, never printed or verbalized— imprisoned by my limited, earthly understanding. Now they were freed, like slaves from my confederate state— unleashed from the big house after years of captivity.

Over there, enlightened faces, joyous children. I heard the clapping of hands. I sensed soul satisfaction. Truly part of it was mine, but it also was the unison rejoicing of travelers I had never met, who had come in contact with my words and music. I never dreamed, when I was bound by skin and contained in blood, that I would ever be able to reach so many beings, so many creatures with my meager scrawlings.

But here it was in all of its splendor—song after song, movement after movement, passage after passage. Everything I had ever written, everything I had ever said, and even everything I had ever dreamed was chorused back at me with the rapidity of a hurricane wind slashing through my essence, penetrating the remnants of all, once me.

I wanted to weep, but laughter besought me.

I wanted to laugh but was overcome by sobs.

I wanted to dance and instead began running.

I ran to the light. I ran to the sound. I ran to the warmth. I ran to the dream. I ran to music and words of my own making. Without fear or trepidation, I ran. I was ushered to a zone, where, behold, all things were made good. Any flaw or error was soaked and cleansed by the grace of generosity and the mercy of benevolence. I heard beauty, and the beauty was mine, and mine was a heart slain by such rapture.

Sitting Five

Oh, my spirit!

Oh my soul!

Oh, breathless wonder that is now my life!

Oh, jubilation that has become my thought, and

Oh, revelation, my constant companion.

I just discovered a new blessing within the spectrum of this rainbow of understanding.

Cascading through the heavens, I was granted the ability to linger. I didn't merely need to bounce and careen from one event to another, but could pause and guzzle, if you will, the experiences of other fellow travelers who had gone on before. I was not concerned with punctuality, just absorbing the lives and times of my kindred spirits who had shed their mortal coil.

Lingering, I found myself in the spirit, within the soul who had been my son. His name was Joshua. During the earthly journey he had been struck down and killed by a careless human. There he was. I knew him, though there were differences. He knew me—a spirit reality. Spiritual in the sense that we were not confined by titles of father and son, but instead, we were fused with a new identity, universal in comprehension.

I was transported with his spirit to the night of his accident. I was with him when his human body was bound to a bed, in a coma. I felt the frustrations of his mind and the soothing dreams that ministered to him in his blackened cave.

My spirit was inundated with fragrance and touch, and I experienced the Eternal Union.

Eternal Union.

I remember hearing people say that after death there is "neither marriage nor given in marriage." I heard people lament that there would be an absence of sexual pleasure.

How limited our thinking as mere bipeds!

Because truly, everything that surfaces in the body is a faint bubble of the intensity erupting in the soul.

All of us knew that sex without love, without tenderness, without passion, was rancored, unfulfilling and repellent. There was a reason we felt this way. The body took all of its cues from the soul. It tried to teach this fragile vessel of skin and flesh how to receive affection by illuminating with sensation.

Doesn't it make sense that the orgasms we were able to achieve in the limited realms of our Neanderthal fleshly comprehension were mere forshadowings of the pleasure conceived in our hearts? So Eternal Union is the pinnacle of pleasure bypassing the limited capabilities of the human form, encapsulating, chilling, shivering, over-whelming joy within the spectrum of the spiritual world—the alpha of all omega.

Unashamedly, unabashedly, I reveled in everlasting sensuality, rattling every fiber of my spiritual space, leaving me to wield back in breathless expectation of the next encounter.

Eternal Union is the eroticism of contentment, eons of consciousness beyond mere human sexuality.

May I say, I became drunk on the spirit of spirits. I was overwhelmed by the vast magnitude of each traveler's depth and the sanctity of their inner treasure.

I felt no embarrassment, as souls would streak across my boundaries, indulging in union with my fancy. I was obsessed with the jubilation of exaltation. Any remnant of dire, human circumstances or senses of dread or memories of lost loved-ones was cleansed by these Eternal Unions.

No regret. No desire to return. No wish to recant the promise of eternal bliss in exchange for the few tender memories of family, friends, acquaintances or lovers.

Sitting Six

I always wanted to meet God.

When I was a child, very small, I thought he would look like Reverend Bacorra, a Presbyterian minister I knew—salt-and-pepper hair, tall, glasses, donning a black robe, wearing oxblood, shiny shoes with scuffed tips.

As I grew older my image changed, but always, I envisioned a physical presence—an actual being.

Now, where was God? I wondered if God was merely light, love and spirit. I smiled at my own ramblings.

Light, love and spirit—not a bad triangle.

Still, I wanted to meet God, face to face, as it were.

I had forgotten that this place had been prepared for me, long before I arrived, so most certainly I was going to receive my audience with my creator, the benefactor of every good and perfect gift that ever came my way. Just when?

Departing from the total release of one Eternal Union, I found myself in a room. The room was perfect to my taste, contingent on my whim, and filled with my concepts of all that was affluent, all regal, and I suppose, even all holy.

Standing, or maybe sitting, or moving a thousand times the speed of light, before me—I don't know which one, and I really don't care—was my image of the Almighty, i.e., God-ala-me. He had once created me in his image, and now the Just of all Justs had consented to being created in my image. He was a marvelous melding of Rev. Bacorra, Jesus, Mary, Virgin of God, a gracious loan officer at my bank, a football coach, my prom date and a thousand other souls and beings who had enriched my life while I was sucking air.

He knew me.

My God—and I mean literally, my God—that's what I yearned for more than anything else in my lifetime—to be known and loved. I was acutely aware that He had been privy to every thought and every deed in my life, from the morbid and sordid, to the brightened and enlightened.

He was God. More—he was *my* God.

He was what He promised to be— the fulfillment of all my plunges at faith; a faith no longer necessary because I had the evidence before my eyes.

"You have questions?" He asked.

His voice was like warm syrup drizzling down the toasted edges of steaming pancakes, rich with creamy butter, smelling of maple.

He was in me, through me, around me. And being spiritual, He was me.

Then, in a brief flash, I was granted insight back into my mortal mind, completely flabbergasted by how confused my brain activity had been. From that befuddled position, I was unable to form any question.

All during my earthly passage, I thought there was so much I wanted to know—so many questions I wanted to "ask God"—but now I had no inquiry— just human thought blubbers. "I don't know what to say."

"Then we shall have a very short conversation."

I laughed. It was a very, very funny retort. And I laughed some more, because I was so delighted to discover that God was as humorous and clever as I had envisioned He should be. After all, how ridiculous to think that the God of all nuance could somehow fail to have as much personality as our human satirists, writers and entertainers.

"What is truth?" I blurted out.

God laughed. It rippled through the sky, creating supernovas in a thousand galaxies and ushering a new dawn on yet a third burgeoning universe. "What is

32

truth, huh?" He mused. "I once knew another man who asked that question, and ended up washing his hands too quickly of the situation before the answer came."

"I'm in no hurry," I smiled.

"Not now. But you were. Everyone is. So that is why truth eludes them. Truth does not cement itself into a temple or a doctrine—it grows. And therefore, anyone who wants to dither here and there to view and possess it usually misses the latest incarnation and ends up worshiping a previously discarded shell."

"We worship. Isn't that truth?"

"All worship is just religion, and all religion is ultimately just the reverence of nature. So the sun shines! People say, God is good. The storms come. They reason, God is speaking or God is angry. Prosperity fills the coffers. God is with us. Poverty and hassle pepper our efforts. God is displeased. Humans have relegated me to atmospheric pressure and barometric rising and falling. It is the earth that humans worship, and the earth is merely something I created, not something I am. So I sent prophets and messengers to take the things of earth and make people understand how truly awesome the universe is—how magnif-icent mercy is over law, grace in

comparison to grit and greed, and crea-
tivity in correlation to repetition or
tradition. So, if they think God is a plant,
may the prophet proclaim my working in
the lily?"

I interrupted. "Are there not any
ways to communicate truth to people in a
sense that they would understand?"

"Let me finish answering your
question about truth. Truth is an
organism. Even in human scriptures,
Genesis is not like Revelation, nor is
Moses like Jesus. There's an evolution
there—a yeast of thinking that shows
truth is ever emerging towards the goals."

"The goals?"

"Acceptance and forgiveness."

"So all truth is acceptance and
forgiveness?"

"Plus a second dimension—the
marriage of emotion and logic. This is
why I created nature. In Eden, I desired a
sanctuary of emotion, because emotion is
the closest the human creation can ever
come to true spirituality. But lacking
focus, they ran from the pure emotion in
pursuit of abstract knowledge. So I gave
them a compromise—logic. Springtime
and harvest. Summer and winter. Day
and night. Cold and heat. An order, if you
will. A natural order."

"So this was good?" I queried.

34

"Do you remember when you were four years old? Ah, wait. You were nearly five, weren't you? And you were so afraid to take the training wheels off your bicycle and roll on two wheels instead of four."

I was gleeful. "Yes, I remember. And I'm so glad you do, too."

"I wouldn't have missed a minute of it. Anyway, you remember how frightened you were to take those wheels off? It's the same way with the human journey. I gave the logic of the natural order—that the threescore and ten year space of time that you live and breathe was meant to be a shedding of dependence upon nature and to stop being afraid of your surroundings. So, like you, removing those training wheels so you could roll faster, independent of restrictions, people could be free of fearing God and could begin to love their world and hopefully one another. In other words, saying to this mountain to be removed—not out of ego nor to see if it actually will happen, but because there are many mountains that stand in the way of human progress and humans finally arriving at acceptance and forgiveness. You speak to those mountains, and they can be removed."

I paused for a moment. I really didn't want to waste time. I think he sensed my dilemma. "This will not be our last conversation. You really don't need to stuff all of your questions into this one session. You are spirit with me now, not limited by time and circumstance, and certainly not paralyzed by impractical codes."

I was relieved. For the first time since my last breath, I realized that although I was a spirit, I was a mere yearling, and there would be much more for me to absorb, including growing to accept and forgive many things I had not yet even considered.

"Just one more question. Why did you kill your son?"

"Which son?" He replied quickly.

"So Jesus is not your son?"

"Jesus is my son. Jesus is my son who was sent with a mission to restore the emotion of spirit ⸫ back to a planet teetering on the brink of destruction because of the rigors of knowledge hunting."

"We are talking about Jesus of Nazareth?"

"When constrained by human body, he was Jesus of Nazareth, but because he was faithful to his mission, he is now Jesus the eternal Son of Man. He still sprinkles his message and mission upon other human souls and gives them the power to become the sons of God."

"Why did you need his blood?"

"You're spirit. Answer the question with the enlightenment that you've received."

I thought. I didn't want to be overly philosophical, nor did I want by any means to come across as ignorant.

"See, I gave you a glimpse into your human mind again, and you were immediately stymied by the fear of how you would look instead of the prospect of joy over what you might discover."

I nodded. It seemed appropriate.

"I kill no one," God continued. "I kill no one. I sacrifice nothing. I give up on not one, single sparrow. Religious people, bound by mere information, free of the spirit of emotion, killed the man, Jesus. He asked me to bring meaning to his sacrifice, to 'forgive them, for they knew not what they did'. So I did what is truly spiritual in all circumstances. I took that which was despicable, cursed, and rancid and turned it into a blessing for them all. Remember, truth is always acceptance and forgiveness."

"Even for murderers?" I asked, really knowing the answer but wanting to hear that wonderful voice say it aloud.

"Especially for murderers."

All at once, I took a deep breath, if such a thing is possible in new world creatures. All I know is that God was inside me, shining beams of light into darkened corners, which moments before, I would have sworn were as brilliant as the noonday sun. I was immediately perfumed—yes, that's the word I want—perfumed by the scent of the mind and spirit of the one that ardent souls call Almighty, and gentler beings deem "Our Father."

I knew at that moment, beyond any darkened misconception, that He would never leave me nor forsake me.

Sitting Seven

I should have asked God if I still have a mind. I was in the presence of the universal Father of all creation, and I was devoid of any question of any depth or any personal value. How difficult would it have been to remember, "Hey God, do I still have a brain?"

Because it sure seems like I'm thinking. As a matter of fact, my mind seems to be tapping resources I never imagined. I'll tell you what it feels like— like I've been plugged in. Some sort of connector was laying flaccid inside me, and now, all at once, I'm engaged. Like a light switch being turned on in a dark room. The revelation of light brought the revelation of everything. Does that make any sense, or do you have to be plugged in?

It's so wonderful, because even as I muse over these ideas, the answers to my questions pop into my being. I think I have it figured out. Of course, it's very simple. As a human being, I was a heart creature—emotional—and my emotions were meant to link to my spirit to gain understanding and purpose. Sometimes, I would actually achieve this. Occasionally I would access an emotional and spiritual conjoining that led me to deeper understanding of my walk and the ways of my world. But what I did not know was that the process needed to be more than a mere flash of exhilarating emotional explosion. The spirit that was in me needed to be connected to my mind, to renew it and energize my faltering thinking with fresh squeezings of juiced-up soulfulness.

I just never put it together. I just believed this was my heart and this was my soul and my mind was some other frontier, only dealing with facts provided.

It does explain one thing. No wonder they told us that we only used a tiny percentage of our brain! Because most of the brain is yearning for a spiritual connection—a hyperlink to the tree of life instead of the tree of knowledge.

So the brain, advertised and touted as the great storer of input, was actually not limited to that at all. Rather, it was hungering and thirsting for spiritual nourishment from both occupant and Maker. No wonder I walked around so perplexed. I was always attempting to rub my two sticks of awareness together, to start a fire in me.

All the knowledge on the earth is not sufficient to construct even the simplest of devices to satisfy the appetite of the human mind. All the wisdom of man cannot construct the wheel. For even basic discoveries were birthed in the blending of spirit and mind—the great coagulation.

So here I am, soaring. Or is it zooming? Or is it standing still in comparison to the speed of others? Whatever—here I am, using my new mind—my renewed mind, my plugged in mind, to reminisce and recall a great conversation I just had with my Creator—my Friend and my God.

It almost overloads the brain, if such were possible.

Flashes of memories. Revelations.

Truth is emotion merged with logic.

Everything culminates in true spirituality, which is always acceptance and forgiveness.

I collide with other traveling souls, sharing my visitation with God, and they rejoice with me.

Then, a difference. I am inexplicably drawn to another being. New. There is something transcendent about the link-up. I allow myself to linger with this one. He speaks to me. "Thank you for stopping," he says.

"Do we ever stop?"

"For so long, I wondered if we would ever start."

There was something here—something I hadn't experienced before. What was it? Yes, what was it that I heard in his tone?

Wait.

I remembered.

A hint of sadness.

I hadn't thought of sadness since, well, since earth. Sadness hangs heavy on the heart unrefreshed. So I asked him, "Why are you so sad?"

"You noticed," he said slowly. "Ahh. Of course you would. I am not sad now. But I was."

"Why were you sad?"

"Because I died and at first gained nothing. Instead I lost—communion with the friends and loved ones who were actually the only soul I possessed. I was left with my own thought."

"But why didn't you just let your spirit reveal to you?"

"Because my spirit wasn't granted revelation. I died not being freed from the restraints of time, but instead living within the passing of moments with no satisfaction, no relief and no revelation."

"My God!" I exclaimed.

"And . . . no God."

I was silenced by his words. I
realized that even during life on earth,
there had always been God. Deny, reject
at will, claim self-reliance freely, but the
presence of God was evident in every
molecule of air and every trickle of light.
Now I was speaking to a soul who had
been to a place—or could it even be a
place?—devoid of Creator.

He perceived my interest, so he
continued. "When I died it was like my
life in the world did not stop, but
continued—but vacant of all the
possessions and people, insight and
blessings which made it tolerable."

"I don't understand," I interrupted.
"When I passed on, time ceased."

"For you. But truly, I discovered
the meaning of that prophetic phrase—
'time is your enemy.' All through my life I
scoffed at the significance of interaction
with people. Don't misunderstand me—I
was not an evil man. I lived by a code of
morals. I occasionally bent that creed but
still maintained a respect for decency and
order. I was possessed with the notion of
planning. Planning my life, planning my
future, planning my family, planning my
business, planning to retire. In the
process of planning, I left no time for
living."

"So if you were bound by time, where did you go? Because there is no time here."

"I went to a place prepared for me. A place that I would have envisioned to be utopia when I walked as a man. It was a place where I was in control. I ruled and I reigned and I was given power to determine my own destiny."

"That seems wonderful . . ."

"Don't be foolish," he interrupted. "The greatest punishment in the world is to grant someone who is empty of true emotion the opportunity to determine quality. I had control. But I had nothing else. The world I created was a whimpering mass of meaninglessness. I was able to accumulate without ever heaping benefit. I was able to visualize but really not know what to see. I heard sounds without music, and I dreamed dreams that always ended, vacant of satisfaction. At first, I persevered. Then gradually, I sank into the doldrums of boredom. And finally, I was left ravaged—inert—useless."

"What was this place?" I asked. I shuddered a bit as I spoke. Nothing seemed more frightening to me than uselessness.

He looked at me. "It was hell. And I don't mean in the sense of a lake of fire, or an island of eternal damnation. But rather, a place prepared for me, where I was forced to subsist on the meat of my own self-worth and drink the dregs of my own insipidness."

Part of me wanted to race away from this horrific tale, but I stayed to ask. "So how did you . . ."

"How did I get here? Because no matter how wretched mankind becomes, God works. He does not recant his blessings simply because we deny him. God makes a way even for the damned."

"What do you mean?"

"I don't know how to explain it exactly. As I was living in my own self-proclaimed inferno of personal excess and dullness, notions began to occur to me. I began to wonder if I might find an exit. Certainly if I were human, I might choose to commit suicide—terminate my misery. Then, there it was. I was granted a simple vision of portals, opportunities for escape. Gradually, one by one, I began to move toward these doors. It was like each one of them quietly requested that I provide some evidence for my worthiness to enter. A question here. A simple test there. I even remember being taken back as a human, alive again, and given an option of choosing a better path. Street people and needy were brought before me—so real that I was able to touch and embrace them. Their vanquished souls were paraded before me, and I was given the gracious opportunity to express humanity. When I was a little boy, they told me of a man named Jesus, who touched the lepers before he healed them. I never fathomed what it meant. I thought it was wild tales told to propagate religious ideas. But here I realized that he touched the decaying forms of these lepers before he healed them to let them know they were loved, even when diseased. I wept. I must have spent weeks, months, dare I say years? Just sobbing over the emptiness in my own soul. And then—another arena. Another place. But I was no longer in charge. At first I resented it, because it was no longer my world, but a world I shared with other souls who were journeying through the anguish of their own inadequacy. We shared a common need as well as a common greed. I found myself going forward, only to rebel against sharing with others to be deposited right back in the same despair. Gradually, portal-by-portal, place-by-place, I found my soul. I never knew I had one. I never allowed myself to believe that there was anything beyond my mind and body. It took me many millennia to make friends with my own spirit and allow myself to discover the depth of true humanity. Which brings me to now."

I smiled at him. "I have good news for you, my friend. You have escaped time."

He smiled at me. "I am no longer grateful for escaping anything. Only yearning to gain more of spirit."

As he spoke these words, the presence that was *he* burst into a beautiful light. It soared upward, dividing into seven glorious beams, one pink, another yellow, a red, a blue, a brilliant orange, an iridescent purple, congealing into glistening amber.

Then he was gone. I paused for a long moment, staring at the last flickerings of his departure.

I contemplated.

God is greater than all ignorance.

Sitting Eight

I thought I might miss time—the pacing of all things. But how irrelevant it is. As I soared throughout the universe, free of constraint, I was perpetually giddy with the loss of control that granted me ultimate authority. Yes, truly, he that will lose his life shall gain it.

In the distance, I saw a great light, what appeared to be a blazing fire, although I felt no heat. It filled the sky with dancing flames and incandescent colors. I was drawn to it, pressing forward. Never in my wildest imagination could I have seen myself heading toward a horizon ablaze. Still, this was purposeful, needed. I came closer. There was no heat at all, but certainly a tugging from the center of this liquid, glistening fireball. All at once, I was within the mass—absorbed.

A completely different sensation.

Where moments before I was unaware of any mass or body, now it was like I once again possessed flesh, blood and bone. And this newly discovered flesh was being yanked, but ever so gently—not as to cause pain—rather, it was as if something was dispelling the excess, trimming away portions that needed to be discarded. I was not frightened or alarmed—just sensitized.

I sought my soul for wisdom, and I heard the comforting voice of understanding. "This is the great cherubim of Eden—the division between the earth as conceived and the world it became. You will enter the cherubim where all the folly of your former existence can be relieved to lighten your load for the eternal pursuit."

Lighten my load? I thought. How much lighter could I get than I had already experienced? Yet it did seem like great burdens were being lifted and indiscretions carved away.

I tumbled, traveling through the great flame, free of heat, free of fear, like a great roller coaster ride, endless, generating new thrills, somersaults, and opening doors to awareness.

I was not alone in the cherubim. There were many souls passing through. Truly we were all being salvaged, escaping through this wall of flames. No dread or discomfort; in fact, a gathering glee over losing the burdensome baggage and tempestuous tantrums of all of earth's care-bound concerns.

Eventually my cleansed soul was birthed from the cherubim and deposited safely on the shore of Adam and Eve's home—Eden.

It was full circle.

That which was born of Eden must return to Eden, for that which was manifested of God was birthed in Eden.

Sitting Nine

Eden is the great amusement park God constructed for humankind to enjoy *being*.

We will never know what we lost until we are allowed to come within its borders and tarry in the expressiveness. The very air is enlivened with spirit. The trees compete for color displaying elaborate foliage. But I think the most beautiful place of all, even nobler than the Tree of Life, is the Garden of Souls.

Every spirit that passes through the cherubim is given the opportunity to come and sit in a great garden, misty with the moisture of memories, and place within that garden the dreams, discoveries, victories and pains of their lifespan. Like a sanctuary of repose for all of earth's treasures, the Garden of Souls affords each human traveler a plot in placement for depositing all the insight of the journey.

I entered the Garden of Souls and sat in the lives of men great and men deemed by earthly standards to be insignificant. I went back into the history of our world and allowed myself to be spiritually present at the birthing of nations. I sat in the Garden of Abraham

Lincoln and was granted a piece of his soul as he freed the slaves and sensed his final thoughts as the bullet from John Wilkes Booth pierced his skull. I entered the earthly life of Jesus of Nazareth as he fed the five thousand, raised his friend Lazarus from the dead, and then collapsed in Gethsemane alone, waiting for nails to pierce his hands and feet, and finally, to rise from the dead. Thomas Edison, Benjamin Franklin, Buddha, George Washington Carver, Susan B. Anthony, Alexander, Joseph, Marie Curie, Mohammed. The list went on and on. It was an indulgence—a living delicacy of my fellows.

I journeyed on and on, into the lives of strangers who became my brothers and sisters through the common gruel and glow of adventure.

And then it was my turn to sit in my own spot—once again, that place prepared for me—and dream and plant. I thought of my sons, Jon Russell, Joshua, Jerrod and Jasson. Those sons I grew to know: Joel, Justin and Daniel. My earthly companions: Janet, Dollie, Steve, James. My brothers Henry, Bill, Dan and Alan. The list went on and on. The afterlife excursion never ceased to amaze me with the diversity of options and the baptisms in rapture.

I stayed on.

I never wanted to leave the Garden of Souls—such a delicious blending of things earthbound and heaven sent. I yearned for all my loved ones to know how amazing it is and how God's great grace is extended.

And then, there it was.

I was called.

I don't know if it was by name or just a sensation that I was needed. But I rose from my garden and headed into Eden.

The Garden of Souls was so enriching.

My next experience would be much different.

Sitting Ten

I fell from the little footbridge and hit the back of my head, on what appeared to be a rusty trash barrel. It was 1957, Delaware, Ohio, at the home of Mrs. Talley, my kindergarten teacher. I went to a private kindergarten because my parents wanted me to begin school and our hometown elementary school had no program. So I was in a private kindergarten in a small class filled with rich kids—my superiors in too many ways.

This was not a dream. This was not a flashback or a memory. I felt my head, and it was stinging with pain, a trickle of blood flowing down my neck from a tiny gash. I was crying as six-year-olds often do when startled by injury.

Laughter. I hadn't remembered the laughter. You see, it was strange. It was like I was living it and recalling it at the same time. I was there, but I was also watching it, and the part of me that was watching it didn't remember the laughter. Why were they laughing? Then I saw the boy standing on the footbridge. He was the one who had pushed me off.

"I guess you don't bounce, fat ass," he said. Renewed laughter from the three or four kids standing nearby.

While I was still mulling his statement, I was transported away to a department store. 1958. I don't know how I knew that, but for some reason the date came to me. I was with my mother, and she was talking to a female sales clerk. The lady spoke. "I'm sorry. We don't carry huskies in pants anymore. There just wasn't that big a demand for them." She looked at me. It was a strange face—a miserable blending of pity, sarcasm and disgust.

The scene changed again. It was 1965. I was standing in line in a locker room. Fifteen, twenty other boys were there. We were all naked. The moist, damp air reeked of the odor of sweat socks and jock straps. One by one we paraded in front of a doctor, puffing on an overstated cigar. He stuck his fingers into our scrotums and asked us to cough. He was rough and coarse, lacking any geniality or courtesy. He stared at each boy's penis and made side comments. It all came back to me. All the fear and apprehension of that moment returned. I was standing there—naked. So much fatter than the other boys. So afraid. It was my turn. I came before the doctor.

He smelled of tobacco and whiskey. His breath was foul with stale garlic. He looked up at me over his glasses, stuck his fingers in me, chuckled and said, "Not much to speak of there." He laughed. The boy next to me, who overheard it, whispered the words down the long chain of my comrades—giggles. I attempted to smile. Flushed with embarrassment and anger, I eased away.

Scene after scene paraded before my eyes.

There was the time I sat in a chair and it broke and the room erupted with laughter. A time that my pants split and there was nowhere to change into others and no place to go and I was forced to hold the seams together with my hands until I went home. There was the laughter of children in the stores, pointing fingers—looks of disapproval.

Awkward moments when in-adequate spacing provided humiliating interludes.

I wanted out of this cavalcade of defeat. I wanted to hide. I didn't understand why this wonderful passage of eternal bliss was being turned into a nightmare of hideous memories.

Then I was sitting in front of a doctor who, as he stared at my belly, told me his diagnosis of trouble with my heart.

I felt no compassion from him, but rather incrimination about my obesity.

Why was I being compelled to relive all this? I had survived. I had weathered the storms of criticism. I had journeyed through life, doing as much as I possibly could with the enlarged frame that burdened me down, trying to hold me back from achievement. Why wasn't I granted a reprieve from this tormented misery?

Wasn't God about acceptance and forgiveness? Wasn't that what He said?

All truth was acceptance and forgiveness.

"All truth is about acceptance and forgiveness." There was a man standing next to me.

"Who are you?" I asked. I peered at him. He was handsome. Blond hair, muscular, bronze skin.

"Who am I?" he responded. "I am you, the you that was never to be, and because you could never be this," he said, pointing at his body, "you refused to accept yourself and never forgave yourself for your inadequacy."

"I didn't want to be perfect," I objected.

"Oh, yes, you did. All things considered, you would never have been satisfied with yourself physically unless you would have become the ideal specimen. So, unable to achieve that status, feeling like you had been cheated out of the opportunity to be handsome and strong, you punished yourself by staying larger than you needed to, fatter than you wanted to be, and criticized more than necessary."

"Why do I need to know this? What value is this to me now?"

"Because you've come to Eden to find the fulfillment of all things. And that includes love. And perfect love has two jobs: first, to accept and forgive. And secondly, to cast out all fear."

"What does being fat have to do with being fearful?"

"You allowed lesser fellows to determine your destiny because you failed to allow yourself the humanity to feel the natural anger and passion. Certainly the anger would have been meaningless to others, but it would have been real and reality is always the first step to rebuking fearfulness."

"So, you are saying I should have gotten mad?"

"No, angry. Anger is the emotion of refusing to accept defeat without a good explanation. You needed to know more—about yourself, about your power and limitations. You accepted without

58

challenge. You agreed without quarrel. You surrendered without battle. Anger is not rage. It is the question formed before frustration totally immobilizes us."

I paused. I didn't totally understand. But, the words touched a lonely spot in my heart. I wept. It felt alien. I thought all my days of blubbering and self-incrimination were over. I was embarrassed by my grief. I felt suddenly and completely abandoned.

And then . . .

There he was.

God.

He took me in His arms and held me and we cried together for a while. He was in no hurry. And I certainly was not willing to leave His embrace.

We lingered.

I cried.

And then God, himself, dried all of my tears.

Sitting Eleven

Light is energy and energy—well, energy energizes things. I always knew this, but I never realized the practical application for that. There is a mission for those who have gone on throughout the universe: to occasionally become the burst of light that produces the energy ushering in strokes of genius and special uncovering within the human scope.

Let me try to explain it to you the way it was unfolded to me.

After I fully emerged from the season of the unveiling of my fears and the cleansing of the terrors of all dread and apprehension, I was given a mission. There are junctures when those who have passed on become a great cloud of witnesses surrounding the events and activities of all planets inhabitable. The purpose of this watch is to intervene with flashes of light.

Now, I know it's hard to understand how a flash of light can produce anything of quality, but light is the element, the natural resource, for all wisdom in the universe—a power supply, if you will. God is light and in Him is no darkness. It is the darkness creeping into the corners of the human soul that fosters the loneliness opening the floodgates to despair, allowing anxiety to taint the human heart.

It is the mission—and may I say, a blessed one—for the universal travelers to pass through the human bodies with flashes of light. To literally enlighten them.

This is why there are times when, as human beings, you can't find your keys, and suddenly you remember. This is the flash of light—a soul who has passed on, streaking through, leaving behind a brief insurgence of intuition, stimulating existing passion and knowledge to greater gain.

Now, please understand, if there is no passion there, nor knowledge, nor desire, the flash of light achieves little. But sometimes, all human beings need is to be enlightened. Sometimes we drive by the person who is stranded by the side of the road, and gradually we become convicted to turn our car around to see if we can help. Our better selves have been enlightened by a soul gone before.

Sometimes we will be in need of an idea and will sit for hours without any notion of how to handle the problem and then there is the flash and the brightened mind will actuate the solution. Sometimes a human soul will be in a hospital room in the middle of the night and will catch a very brief glimpse of a glowing image at the end of their bed and will feel strengthened and encouraged by the visitation.

This is what the Eternals call a *eulophaisian*. It is a visitation of light into the human spirit to energize existing powers, strengths, and insights that have grown dormant through either fear or despair.

It is what causes the captain of a boat to pull up short of entering a channel of water teeming with danger. It's what causes us to turn right instead of left and in so doing, engage a miraculous blessing. It's what causes a mother to go and check on her child in the middle of the night to find the child is sick or not breathing well.

It is the extra flash of light piercing the human spirit, awakening the natural gift of sensory perception suppressed by the commonality of repetition.

I took my stint and instituted many *eulophaisians*. Each blessing granted to me in this world beyond flesh, seems to be greater than the last. But certainly to pierce my fellow human with the light, and to see sensibility alerted, was almost too magnificent for words.

Humans, you are not alone.

You are never manipulated, nor controlled.

You are never without free-will choice, but because of the wisdom of your creator, and the power of light, you are granted a *eulophaisian*—an opportunity for flashes of illumination to enlighten your better selves.

Sitting Twelve

Back when I paid a monthly electric bill to be "lit up," well, back then I just never liked angels—prissy and prudey. People would tell me "angels were watching over me." It kinda gave me the creeps. How annoying would it be to have some prissy and prudey creature watching over you? How could they avoid being critical and fussy? I never got the wings and the harp thing either. Angels praised God all day—sounded like the most boring thing I ever heard.

Now that I have passed on, I've encountered angels. They are anything but prissy and prudey and certainly not boring.

Angels are everlasting fellows granted a human sense of free will and fair play. When we pass on, we cease to be concerned about free will and fair play, because, frankly, all will is possible and all play is fair. But the angels have the mission of connecting with humans on whatever planet and bringing about specific changes. So the old saying that we've all entertained angels unaware is not only true but also very practical.

There are times eulophaisians are not enough to provide the benefit and care necessary to protect people from danger and destruction. A man in a desert can have a eulophaisian all day long, but it won't bring him water. Events cause God to use his angels to inhabit human form, performing the tasks others would do if they were able to be there.

Understand this; angels are never dispatched unless God believes the human heart would have met the need if it could have been possible for humans to be available for such an endeavor. And angels are hot on their job. They petition God on behalf of humans. They are enthralled by human existence and often saddened because they are unable to assist because human compassion has dwindled to such a degree that God cannot allow intervention without superseding the sanctity of free will.

So in seasons of despair, it may seem despair increases.

Also, angels, being spirits, don't have bodies of their own. So they must find those willing humans who have some natural, intrinsic ability to comprehend extra-terrestrial mission, who will allow themselves to be reinvented for a brief season to become the caretakers of angelic proceedings.

Matter of fact, if I were to go back as a human being today, my first instinct would be to let the Universal of Universes know I was ready to be possessed by a spirit supernal. I would open my eyes and ears to all things contentious and be prepared to intervene for a heavenly cause.

But . . .

There have been times in the history of mankind when the conscience of humanity became so darkened that angels were unable to intercede. Just as our faith makes us whole, it is our hope that makes us angelic. During those seasons, the angels intercede in music for mankind. Yes, when angels wish to inspire humans to acts of charity they use the power and emotion of music to reach the soul and stimulate the conscience. Just as a fine wine intoxicates the mind and body, music imbibes the heart and soul to enact deeds beyond normal reaction.

Because as tragic as the events may seem throughout history, there is always a saving grace to pull us from the depths of destruction and despair. For every Napoleon there is a Wellington; for every Hitler there is a Churchill. And for every Caesar there must be a Christ, or the world would catapult into utter darkness.

Angels are always looking for souls who are ready to believe the spiritual can overcome the impractical.

Angels are the ultimate messengers of God because they inhabit the flesh and blood of his prized creation.

Sitting Thirteen

I found God alone, if such were possible, in the corner of Universe 2, reflective. Sensing my presence, he spoke.

"Dawrus is his name. A lion. Fierce and tender all at the same time. He was hungry. The rains had failed to replenish the grasslands. Less water, less grass, less grazing, less wildlife—a cycle. Tanyee was an antelope—graceful, daring, gentle and, well, vulnerable—a bit of a bend in a front leg. The others in the herd protected her, keeping her in the center, but as I said, Dawrus was hungry and on this day, Tanyee was slower, unable to keep up with her own protection. Dawrus caught her, killed her and ate her. He felt a sadness in his efforts but a necessity to his purpose. Survival. I understand the process. I just miss Tanyee."

I remained silent.

Even God needs a chance to grieve.

Sitting Fourteen

Some called it Bertolas, others Veracholbi, another emoted the name Quan, while many exuded more an impression—Pensoral. My perceptions were much more child like. In my heart, I referred to it as *spirit world*. I know it sounds silly, but I saw no need to pursue any pretension about names and such.

So allow my simple interpretation.

Spirit world: a place—no not exactly a place—not in the conventional sense of occupying acreage or miles, but a location gaining depth and density because living souls—translated beings—congregated here to consider the wonders of the universe.

Awe.

Spirit world is an actual happening, if you will. Now, follow this. Here, the real world is spirit, and the supernatural is the physical world surrounding us. For you to understand, you must comprehend that as humans, we live in a physical existence dependent upon and subject to our senses. Our poets and prophets tell us of another world, intangible, wherein dwell the better angels of our thinking, the souls of our loved ones who have passed, and the very throne of God.

We often crinkle our brows, trying to comprehend this world beyond because it is inaccessible to our senses.

We are bemused by the whole concept.

But in spirit world it is exactly the opposite. Virtues like understanding, compassion, love, tenderness, and reasoning are tangible while a shadowy form of a physical world looms far in the distance, only conjured by the excellent discourse by some soul's interpretation of such matters.

That's right. Someone describes a mountain, valley, river or an ocean—they perceive—beyond our spiritual sight, and we all, as it were, close our eyes, and try to envision such a physical anomaly. It's enough to make me laugh right out loud.

I've come to spirit world, or was it compelled? Certainly brought. Anyway, I'm here to discuss with these wonderful spirits what we call the chemistry of intervention. Because free will exists throughout the universe, intervention from the spirit world must be sensitive to that creative mandate—meticulously dis-cussed and determined.

Does this make any sense? Well, of course, I will not make complete sense because this is the world of the spirit—an existence dependent upon the union of emotion and logic.

I just continue to learn. During my mortal impasse, I thought there would come a time when I would be infused with all knowledge and become one with the universe—a gift, as it were.

But that is not the way it is. We were always best as beings when enlightened instead of just lit up. So the afterlife—what a strange name for it— maybe better phrased, the actual life—is a learning experience, but with one very important difference. The learning is retained, never to be forgotten again.

Case in point. Names ceased to be important. Everything is registered on an emotional level. So one soul intertwining with mine seemed to be named Calm because that's what I felt when they were in my presence. Another was Energy. Still another Warmth. I really appreciated Understanding. Levity, of course, made me laugh, though possessing a serious side.

I was wondering who I was to these fellow travelers. One shared that I was perceived to be Smile. I liked that. Of all the emotions evoking an expression, Smile seems to be one of the nicer colleagues.

I learned so much in spirit world.

For instance: the universe and the creatures within, no matter how diversified, share four common parts of their being. Each creation possesses a heart, a soul, a mind and a strength.

Throughout the entire expanse of the heavens, every created being also partakes of the same four elements: blood, water, fire and air.

Parallels—the blood so much like the strength. The air like the soul. The fire so much like the mind and the water so much like the heart.

So all creation bleeds, thirsts, breathes and needs warmth.

How fearfully and wonderfully we are made.

While human, morals and ethics were debated with fervor. It is not so in spirit world. In the world of spirit, there are only three parameters: a trio of questions asked to determine the value of any decision.

Number one: Is it an action of faith?

Number two: Is it a vision of hope?

Number three: Is it a movement of love?

Please note, while created beings tend to be subjective, looking on the outward appearance, our Creator only looks on the heart, unconcerned with the things of our flesh.

I discovered that the universe, although filled with books and inspired volumes, has only one word that invokes the term *HOLY*. And though there are many indiscretions and flaws causing the demise of created beings, there is only one vice deemed *SIN*.

The virtue of all virtues? EVOLVE.

The abomination of all desolation— STAGNATE.

For when all is said and done, the true spirit of God is a breath of wind blowing across our hearts, cajoling us to repent. To change. To evolve.

And the only darkness that exists throughout the universe of universes is the arcane rhetoric that anything, anyone or any belief can remain the same.

If we are evolving, there is nothing to defend, nothing to protect, nothing to struggle against and nothing to fight for; just a willingness to receive the newness of fresh thinking.

But if we stagnate, a banner is raised over an existing belief and must be guarded and honored above all else, defended for the sake of posterity—if necessary, to the death.

Patriotism is stagnation, bruised by arrogance, looking for an offending party.

War is nationalism cornered by an unexpected reality.

Ignorance is the offending party that fearfully ushers in the latest unexpected reality.

Patriotism, war, ignorance and fear—the quadrangle of ultimate deception.

I'm so glad I was given the opportunity to receive. The next interaction would be much more difficult, demanding all the emotion and reasoning within my soul.

Sitting Fifteen

The chemistry of intervention: it is the passion of every spirit being to honor creation by blessing the created.

But as I stated earlier, there are rules. Guidelines for intervention.

The spirit world can enter the physical world in only two arenas: inspiration and natural science. Of course, spirits cannot simply pass along data that would inspire, or scientific formulas to cure disease and solve the ailments of planets. No, there needs to be a delivery system. This is where it gets complicated.

The delivery systems that bring about inspiration and science happen to be two conditions which all created beings despise.

For I discovered the only way the spiritual world can pass along the inspiration creating ideas is through *hassle*.

That's right. The natural world has to cause the planeters to pause long enough and be troubled by something strongly enough that they seek a new answer, instead of repetition.

Without hassle, there is no inspiration for ideas. But because people hate hassle and fear having the routine interrupted, they tend to shut down and become frustrated instead of opening their minds and their hearts to new ideas.

Why would we ever pursue an electric light bulb if candles burned perfectly? Who would have ever considered constructing an automobile if one horsepower got the job done? Why would we have made the simple pencil if tiny chunks of charcoal could make thin lines?

Hassle is what the Creator uses to make blessing. Without it, there would be no ideas because discovery would be impossible and intervention, as I said, forbidden.

Placed into the crust, core, and the atmosphere of every planet, are all the elements necessary to make that civilization survive and thrive in prosperity, free of disease. Isn't that remarkable?

My dear companion, Understanding, put it this way. "Each planet is a treasure chest, waiting to be unlocked to reveal the wisdom in making them self-contained, self-motivated and self-aware."

But, like any treasure chest, there is a lock that demands a key. The key? *Labor.*

Oh, how all creatures both great and small, rebel against the rigors of work. Instead of celebrating the pursuit of knowledge through research, the discovery of inventions through per-spiration, they pursue shortcuts and literally struggle to find new excuses for leisure. Leisure conceives slothfulness, breeding avarice and gluttony, birthing vice.

A true statement. No one ever worked himself to death.

It was during this discussion of the chemistry of intervention that I found myself torn between two very strong emotions. One was feeling greatly amused over the simplicity of our dialogue. The other was frustration because my knowledge of human behavior made it seem as if our task was insurmountable.

How could you ever get humankind to welcome hassle and labor? They abhor both of them. Meanwhile, cures await.

My new friend, Perception, put it this way: "Is there anything throughout all the universe, that was believed to be one way in one generation that still is accepted in the next generation in totality? No. Each generation must take the wisdom of their predecessors and find the folly in the logic, insert new truth, energize it, and gingerly pass it along to their children, knowing that they will have to do the same."

Levity made us all laugh by summing up his feelings by saying, "I think the only answer is more flat tires and cold coffee."

As silly as that was, we understood that as spiritual beings, we were dealing in the deepest realms of practicality. I do recall faint memories of my journey when, as a human, I believed myself to be so complex. Now that I am in the spirit world, I understand how simple and delightfully uncomplicated human life was meant to be.

There really was always only one danger: to be too blessed and lulled into a stagnancy that would ultimately lead to personal decline.

What were those words? Ah, yes. God chastises those He loves. If by chastising, you mean hassles and work, then you're right.

He really does love us.

Sitting Sixteen

A duo of unlikely spirit friends called me aside. It was personal; the two I knew as Calm and Confrontation. Paired, they seemed to be a contradiction, but I listened.

Calm spoke first. "Can we have a moment with you, Smile?"

I did. Smile, that is. My name was a little silly but did have an endearing quality. "Sure," I said.

"There are some things we need to talk about," piped Confrontation.

His spiritual voice was not nearly as comforting as Calm but certainly gained my attention.

Calm continued. "For each of us, there comes a time when, in order to honor evolution, we must examine our own life."

"It won't just be one time," said Confrontation.

"True," agreed Calm. "But the first time, well, the first time can be the most, let's say . . . difficult."

It gave me pause. I wasn't afraid. Still, I wondered.

Confrontation jumped in. "You see, each of us left our mortal lives with many unanswered questions. Many conflicts unresolved. Many needs unfulfilled. You see, Smile, you just can't come into Eternity and think that all of these are going to be wiped away like some sort of clean slate. Each one of us needs to feel victory in our own souls. Each one of us needs understanding of our own appetites"

"I can see that," I said.

Calm took a deep breath. "You died a fat man. Do you know why?"

"And here I thought it was because my heart stopped," I jabbed, trying to lighten the moment.

"The emotional heart can stop too, you know," Confrontation jabbed back at me.

"I don't understand," I said.

"What Confrontation means is that sometimes, just like the physical heart can suffer blockage, not permitting the blood to circulate well, the emotions can be clogged, leaving us little room to feel."

I was a bit exasperated. "I'm sorry. I don't know what you two are trying to get across to me."

Confrontation fired back. "You see? The minute we start talking about you—your inadequacies—you become angry."

"I'm not angry."

"Then tell us how you would describe where you are," Calm asked.

I took my own deep breath. "I guess I've been enjoying myself so much that I really don't understand why I should go back and discuss the problems I thought were all left behind."

"It would be great if the problems were left behind, if they didn't affect your spirit," chimed Confrontation. "But they did. So many of those insecurities and frustrations live on. They survived your body and still dwell in your heart."

"Why didn't you promote your music and books more?" Confrontation kept on.

"I don't know. I guess I thought it was enough to just write them."

"Were you afraid to promote them?" pursued Calm.

"Afraid?"

"Yes, afraid," challenged Confrontation. "As long as they were just curlicues, dots and letters on a piece of paper you could believe they were great—wonderful. But the minute they left your hands and fell under the scrutiny of your fellow man, well, then there was always the danger of rejection."

"Are you saying I feared rejection?" I asked sincerely.

"Perhaps that was the reason for remaining fat all your life," Calm suggested.

"I don't get it," I protested. "How could being fat all my life keep me from rejection? Didn't my obesity bring on rejection?"

"Perhaps," Confrontation asserted. "But it also gave you a reason for calling people bigots because they didn't accept you, while still being able to escape the real critique of your work. You could always say they didn't like you because you were fat."

I stopped. I felt no need to argue with these two brothers in spirit. There was no condemnation, just legitimate, tender concern.

Calm seized the moment. "Each one of us has fear. And once produced, it manufactures all sorts of excuses, which ultimately become reasons why we persist in our own personal failure and cease to evolve. Smile, your fat wasn't evil, but your fat was caused because you were afraid. Afraid to compete, at times afraid to participate, so your fat led to a terror which caused you to stagnate."

"And that," I concluded, "is really the only sin."

Calm agreed .And Confrontation nodded.

The end of my first session. I knew I would return many times. More fear to address, stagnation to confront, and burdens to unload.

Sitting Seventeen

A problem amiss.

I had not felt this way since I had died. I was just soaring along, and then, there it was. At first, I didn't recognize it—emotionally obtuse to my newfound being. But a faint memory of what and how it was began to return.

Regret.

My God, what was it? Faded memories of mistakes, miscalculations, foibles, entered my mind.

Then I was in a room. Something was displaced. I felt confined in this space, boxed in, beautiful music playing, and a fragrance—not odious, floral, but ever so slightly stale, with a voice singing, unable to determine the words. Conversations nearby, but once again the content escaped me.

And then, something terrifying—I seemed to be regaining features, shape, circumference and depth. I hadn't felt my own physical presence since my Earth time. But now there was the reinstatement of all tangible—a physical world.

Chairs. I was sitting. My arms and legs forming before my eyes, the plumpness of my being returning to vex me.

Someone next to me. I could see him. He had form—a strikingly debonair fellow. Jealousy pierced my heart, nasty, foul.

I wanted out of this dream. Or whatever it was.

"May God be praised," said my handsome visitor.

I nodded, too stunned to speak.

"Jonathan. That's your name, right?"

That was my name. But it seemed odd, a trifle clichéd.

"Jonathan, right?" he pursued.

I nodded, sluggishly.

"God has been good to all of us."

"Yes, He has," I returned, quietly.

"It is a great gift He has given us. Life, eternal life." My friend was warm and understanding. I felt comforted by his words.

"Yes, it is a great gift," I agreed.

"I think that's why I love to praise him," the stranger continued. "There's just something about praising and worshipping God that makes you feel— well, that makes you feel good all over. Just to be in His presence and know that He is God and He is powerful and He is come to give us new life."

These were wonderful words. I felt greatly reassured, even though I sat there in my original human form, inadequate as it was. I was comforted.

The companion continued, "Sometimes I just get, well, I just get overwhelmed by God's goodness. I feel enlightened on a path of discovery. I want to sing. I want to clap my hands. I want to bow my head. I want to pray. I want to fast. I want to show Him and everyone else how much He means to me. Oh, my dear friend, Jonathan, why can't the world see how good it is to believe?"

I shook my head. "I don't know. I've wondered that myself."

"Sometimes," he continued, "I just want to go out and tell them all about how important it is to come and worship together, bow and pray, give your tithe, and fellowship with people who believe and think like you do."

I nodded my head again, and he continued again.

"Why can't people see? Why are they so blind? Why do they refuse to repent of their sins? Why won't they walk the paths of righteousness? Why do they do the things they do?"

"I guess, because they don't understand."

"They don't understand, Jonathan, because they need a teacher, a voice, a cleric, a prophet, a seer. They need a shepherd to lead them to the green pastures. For, after all, we are not merely individuals, but a body. A body of believers, a corporation, an idea, a fellowship united in a common good against a desperate evil."

"Evil?" I asked.

"Yes. Sin. Immorality. Competition. Spiritual wickedness in high places. The powers of darkness. Governments standing against the very will of God. Ignorance of the better way. People who need our liberty—oh, yes— they are jealous of our power and freedom, living lives of degradation. Committing acts of abomination and immorality. Jonathan, we have a job. To bring the right way to these people—a new product, an improved brand of existence. To cleanse them from all unrighteousness."

"Isn't that God's job?"

"We are God's hands. We're the only God that some people will know. If we do not teach them the paths of truth, and get them to agree—yes, wherever two shall gather in agreement, it shall be done—then they will be lost."

"Well, aren't we all a little lost?" I queried.

"Lost, but now found, dear comrade. No longer bound by the constraints of sin. We have the goods. We are more than conquerors and therefore not subject to the degradation of these lesser beings. He has called us to preach to them and change them and make them any way we can into followers and to worship. Ah, yes. Worship."

"But don't we worship God by living lives of love?" I was growing concerned; yet somehow felt I was in the wrong to be so suspicious.

"Love, yes, love. For God so loved the world that whosoever believeth shall be saved, but whosoever believeth not shall be damned. Our God is a consuming fire."

"And He's light. And love," I punctuated.

"Yes, truly, Jonathan, God is love. But He expects us to give. Oh, I don't care what it is, as long as it is sacrificial— fasting, intercessory prayer, reciting the rosary, baptism, immersion, sprinkling or pouring, devotions, studies, fund-raisers, praying to the East, finding Nirvana, long retreats where we learn the depth and breadth of the power of God and those commandments which He demands we follow in order to curry His favor." He had entered another realm—driven and delirious.

I was feeling flustered and trapped, guilt-ridden and inadequate. I wanted to leave. I wanted to shed this old body and return to my spiritual journey. I peered at my friend more closely. He was transforming before my eyes. The features, though still chiseled with some attractive attributes, were aging, wrinkling and becoming ashen. His suit, once white, or perhaps cream, had now turned smoky gray.

He continued his spiel. "Where is your sin, Jonathan? How will you serve God? What will you give up for heaven's sake? Who will you witness to today about your faith? How will you help us reach the heathen in the foreign lands? How much are you willing to give? Do you understand the depravity of man?"

Question upon question. The regret I felt now was anguish and despair. "I would like to go. Please. Just let me go."

The stranger grabbed me by the hand. "Don't run away, sinner. Almost art thou persuaded to be a believer? All you have to do is fall down and worship. That's right. Just fall down and give up. Let go and let God and let worship. Cast aside your humanity and all your pride and fall down and worship."

He was tugging on my arm, pulling me to the ground. I didn't know what to do, so I screamed at the top of my lungs, "Lord, save me!"

"Hell awaits. Believe me—Hell awaits." He was so close I could smell his putrid breath. I closed my eyes, recoiling, falling face down in despair and rage.

All at once the scene changed. Lying very still I could hear the chirping of a single bird. I peeked from my prostrate retreat. Home. I was in the expanses of the heavens, floating, feeling the cool breezes of Eternity sweep across my fevered soul.

Then the Voice, his voice. "Are you all right?"

I knew that gentle timbre. It was my Creator, the Lord. My friend and fellow-spirit.

"Yes, I mean no. Well, I think . . . I will be. What was that?"

"That was a room built by man, attempting to imprison my spirit."

"What was it called?"

"It's called religion."

"And who was the stranger? The man talking to me?"

"You probably know him—or at least have heard of him. He was once a friend. His name is Lucifer."

Sitting Eighteen

The planet's name was Rhilea.

I was sent there to be the ruler for a season. I know it sounds ridiculous, for me to be ruler, but it was part of the process.

Rhilea was a beautiful planet, filled with, well, filled with humans. At least, the way I remembered humans. There were distinct differences. Rhileans were not a warring sort. They were industrious and intelligent. I didn't even know why I had been sent to be with them.

They were totally comfortable with my arrival, me being the third earth spirit who had visited them and walked amongst them as leader. I felt inadequate to the task. But they seemed unfamiliar with pride and arrogance at being instructed by another. It soon became evident what my mission was on their planet. Because as industrious, intelligent and peace loving as the Rhileans were, they had no art or music. There was no tuneful melody and harmony to fill in the spaces of their day.

Having never lived in a world without music, without art, I was astounded to see what a vacuum was created by its absence. There was still

family, friendships and human interact-
tion, just no soundtrack or creative visual
aid to the ongoing discourse and drama.
Since there was no music, there were no
instruments and no dance. There was no
paint. The walls and the buildings were
all wood or stone, which meant that they
were only the colors found in nature.

Lovers fell in love without song

People were married without dance.

I was in an immediate quandary,
because although I knew how to compose
music, I knew nothing about making
instruments or art supplies to begin
programs among the people.

About the time I was going to hatch
a big, huge apology and then run away,
several fellow spirits arrived in Rhilea to
work with me, to be a part of my Cabinet,
as they put it. They were craftsmen and
inventors and artisans of all types and
styles. Soon, from their skilled hands, we
had a piano. I resumed my composing as
other artisans constructed other
instruments, mixing and mingling paints
and colors, etching and chiseling the
marble forming statues, instructing the
young Rhileans in movement and acting.
These students became the first
generation of dancers and thespians.

Other spirits arrived to inspire with
technique and style of architecture. It was

an amazing sight, the foundling of a creative heritage. And it was so quick. In no time, bands were playing, orchestras performing, painters painting, art displayed, sculptors sculpting, statues erected, plays and ballets presented.

The sweet grimness once displayed on the faces of the long-suffering Rhileans was soon replaced by the joyful and tearful countenances of a rallied people. Time passed—a generation or more. The performers became artisans and then masters.

I was needed no more.

I quietly slipped away to a planet called Terra Sabea.

There I dwelled among a people whose souls had so much, yet lacked the simple joy of comedic thinking and an ability to find a sense of humor in life. I stayed on until laughter became the national pastime.

On I journeyed, being afforded the privilege and the responsibility of ruling and reigning. I moved in and out of the constraints of time. Mine was truly the best of both worlds.

Sitting Nineteen

Something is wrong.

Ever since I left my last assignment I have felt—I don't know—sluggish. If I were on earth, I'd call it being run down, tired, needing a nap. But not here. At least, not up until now. I almost feel achy. Yes, a dull achiness plagues me.

Sounds.

Voices.

But it isn't Calm or Confrontation.

Certainly not the voice of God.

Mumbling.

Please be quiet.

How maddening hearing words you cannot quite ascertain.

Yes, be quiet.

The soreness again.

I feel it in my head but, no, I don't have a body.

Why do I feel so leaden? Logy. Yes, that was the word. It's like my whole being is cement, drying.

If I could just focus for a second. There are no seconds. I never had to focus before. Why now?

A smell. What's that smell? I know that smell.

More voices. Mumbling murmurs.

What is the smell? I do know that smell . . .

Wait. Someone's calling me.

The smell is stronger.

It smells like...can't place it. But, someone's definitely calling me. I am so tired and most certainly feeling . . . now it's a pain . . . in my head. Yes, in my head. I must have a head.

What's that smell?

I remember it from when I was a kid. What was it? Some sort of...an antiseptic?

"Jonathan . . . Mr. Cring . . . "

That's me. At least, that was me. "Only Lucifer calls me Jonathan."

"Excuse me?"

"Oh, my head."

"Mr. Cring. Mr. Cring."

"Mr. Cring regrets to inform you that he will no longer be able to attend this life. His new name is Smile."

There were more mumbles. Two, maybe three voices. A pungent, powerful odor right in front of me.

"Oh, my God. What was that?"

"Mr. Cring. Are you there? Wake up. Mr. Cring. Mr. Cring."

All the reluctance and weariness surrendered and became pain. My head throbbed. My throat was dry, raspy and very sore. "What is this?" I said. "Where is God?"

"He's hallucinating." A voice intoned.

"God is hallucinating?" I inquired. "That must be wild." My speech seemed slurred, but the statement, I thought, quite funny.

"Mr. Cring. Mr. Cring. Mr. Cring." The voice got louder with each repetition.

I mustered all my strength and I yelled as loud as I could. "What do you want?" As I did, suddenly my eyes popped open.

Yes, my eyes.

I found myself in a foggy white room, surrounded by people in blue garments, fully masked. The pungent smell was all around me. Now I recalled. Alcohol—that was the smell. Alcohol.

"Mr. Cring. Mr. Cring. Are you all right?"

I wasn't. Wherever this was, it wasn't good. Whatever was going on was bad. And wherever this new mission was taking me was far from the comfort I had grown accustom to. "Tell God I'm going to pass on this one and save it for the next spirit council," I croaked.

Suddenly I felt a pain in my hip. Yes. I once again had a hip. There was someone standing over me, lightly slapping my face, looking right into my eyes. "Are you there, Mr. Cring? Are you there?"

"I told you. I'm not Mr. Cring. Mr. Cring does not live here anymore. But I will be more than happy to forward a message."

The pesky observer continued to pursue. "Jonathan Richard Cring, we need you to wake up. You are in a hospital room, and we need you to wake up."

Groggy, unable to comprehend the message. I was a prime minister of planets, a composer of universal music. I'd had an audience with Him—Jonathan Richard Cring had already done his thing.

"Jonathan?" This was a female voice. I tried to look and see where the voice was coming from. It seemed to be all around me. "Jonathan?" she repeated.

It sounded like someone I knew—if they had taken Quaaludes and were in a really big cave. I tried to focus. The voices continued, many of them now—a common theme. They all knew my name and for some reason, they all wanted me to wake up.

"I don't know what this mission is," I said. "But really, I'm not trying to be resistant. Whatever the spirits want to do is great by me. I just feel kind of sleepy."

A hearty laugh filled the room. "I think he's going to be okay," said one of the more basal surrounders.

■■■

It was the next morning when I fully regained consciousness.

I was not dead.

I had been in a coma for two weeks in the hospital. No one knew why I went under, or how I got back.

There was a series of tests to make sure all vital organs were responding, and everyone seemed pretty satisfied I was fairly solid.

But I wasn't.

I had full memory of being a spirit, of chatting with God, traveling the universe free of time.

To merely say I did not want to be Mr. Cring again would be an understatement.

I was ripped from my real home and placed back in the orphanage created by my birth.

I laid my head back and tried to sleep.

Maybe, if God was merciful, He would let me come back home.

Sitting Twenty

Motionless, thoughtless, dreamless, more or less just a night's sleep.

I awakened in the morning, my bedside surrounded by family and friends. Each face was a book of information, filled with a story of woe and concern. I could barely stand to glance at them. I loved them all, but they were no longer mine, nor was I theirs.

I was a stranger to this land. Maybe it was one of those . . . *mortalations* . . . that I had heard about during my death. Maybe I was lifted out—transplanted—to this new existence. Yet, as I recall, the human soul going through mortalation is oblivious of transformation, and I am certainly tragically aware.

I lay there staring at the ceiling, trying to avoid meeting the probing gazes of my loved ones.

The doctor walked into the room. "Good morning, Mr. Cring, how are we feeling?"

"We are dead," I said flatly.

"No, I don't believe so, although you did have us worried for a while. You were in a coma. We are not quite sure what caused it . . . you are a diabetic, so there

may be some related cause, but we're not
sure."

I remained silent. One by one my
family and friends came to express their
wishes and concerns. Honestly, it all just
blended into a gigantic "I'm-so-glad-
better-hope-feel-good-soon-love-get-well"
mantra.

I guess I was depressed.

I had a whole new insight on
Lazarus, whom Jesus raised from the
dead. No wondered Jesus told them to
unbind him and let him go. Lazarus was
certainly in no hurry to come out of the
tomb. It's just not fair to kill a guy and
then indiscriminately bring him back to
life.

Yes, I was certainly despondent. Or
maybe just human again. That would do
it.

I needed to talk to someone. If I was
ever going to resume whatever it was I
was supposed to do, I probably should
find out how crazy I am or at least, how
crazy they're going to believe I am.

I decided not to talk to my friends
or family. I didn't want to get into some
sort of competition about why I told this
one and didn't tell that one. You can see,
it could turn into a real mess.

I asked the hospital administration
if they could have a Catholic nun come

and see me. I don't know exactly why I picked a nun. I think it's because they seem to be very docile and quiet, and I think they might be able to listen for a long time without commenting. Of course, the fact that I'm not Catholic might be detrimental—but you take your best shot.

About three hours later, after scooting all of my visitors from the room my little Catholic nun arrived. She was younger than I had hoped, but still adequately sheepish and seemed to have a good set of ears behind her black bonnet.

She introduced herself as Sister Mary Ann Jennings. We exchanged a few pleasantries, and then I began.

"Sister Mary Ann, I would like you to listen to my story. Please do not be frightened for my sanity. They have given me a clean bill of health. I just need someone to hear what has happened to me."

She patted my hand and said, "The Lord be with you."

"You see, Sister Mary Ann, that's part of the problem. The Lord has been with me, and I have been with Him. And I'd really like to go back."

She was already perplexed.

A natural reaction. I'm sure they had not rehearsed this at the convent.

I proceeded to tell her my story. I told her about death and the absence of time. About acceptance and forgiveness. About the spirit world, about ruling and reigning on planets. About discovering that Lucifer was the priest to all religion.

She stood quietly except for occasionally shifting her feet—I assume fatigue, or perhaps a split decision over whether to race for the door.

I plunged onward. "And then, I heard them calling me back. But I don't really want to be back. I mean, I love everyone here. Probably more than ever before, but I feel my mission is done. I feel there is nothing left for me to do."

Then, all at once, this little waif of a girl looked at me and said, "If your story is true and you've been with God and He sent you on missions to other planets to rule and reign, why have you chosen to dig your heels in on being commissioned to return to our planet?"

I was stymied. She was right. I certainly didn't object to anything else. So why now?

"I guess," I began, "being alive again makes all the rest of it seem like just a phony dream."

"And this would be a dream you've had before?"

It may have been my imagination, but she suddenly seemed to have donned an Irish brogue. Maybe it was real; maybe it was my desire to place a characterization upon her. Considering my recent revelations, who would know?

"No," I said. "I have never had this dream before."

"Then who's to say it's a dream, let alone a phony one?"

"You mean you believe me?"

"No, I think you're a little teched. I'd like to scurry back to the convent and have my evening potato soup. But it's not for me to decide such things."

I smiled. "So, what do you think I should do?"

"Not tell your story a lot," she said, smiling herself.

"Why do you think I'm here?"

"That's easy," she said. She patted my hand and headed towards the door.

"Well?" I asked.

She turned to me at the door and said, "You're here because you're not there."

With this, my little nun pushed on the door, walked out and disappeared.

I felt like a little boy at a Chinese restaurant, who opened his fortune cookie and realized there was no fortune inside.

"I'm here because I'm not there?"

Meanwhile, my nurse enters with a nighttime sleeping medication.
Maybe it's my pill back to God.

Sitting Twenty-One

That night I dreamed.

I thought I was back in eternity, but it was bizarre. Kind of like a Milton Bradley version—overly commercialized and certainly low budget. I found myself once again standing before God. He was different.

God had a body; he was shorter, and looked and talked like Groucho Marx. "So, what brings you into the presence of Me, the Almighty?" he said, puffing on a large purple cigar.

"God?" I inquired.

"Say the word and get two hundred and fifty dollars."

"You seem so unusual."

"You think I'm unusual, you should see my brothers. One of them thinks he's an angel . . .that's why we call him Harpo . . ."

I was so disappointed.

God was doing a burlesque routine in my dreams, with lousy material.

So that meant three things.

I was not in heaven.

I was not talking to God.

And if I was responsible for the set-ups, I was no longer a very good writer.

"Don't be so hard on yourself," Groucho God said. "You should have seen some of the sketches I worked when I was in the Catskills. Actually, to tell you the truth, that cat had no skills . . ."

He flicked his cigar and I chuckled. "God, why aren't I in heaven?"

"Looking over your record, I think you should be very happy with this ten minute interview . . "

"Is this all a mortalation?"

"If I knew what a mortalation was I would answer. But since I don't, let me just flip my cigar. That's pretty funny by itself, don't you think?"

I sighed. What I needed was a spiritual *kick*, not *shtick*. I began walking away, and as I did, Father Marx said, "Hey, kid. It's all up to you, ya' know. Whether it begins today or tomorrow, it's all up to you."

As he spoke the last word, the morning nurse shook me. "Mr. Cring, it's time for you to wake up."

"I'm not dead?" I asked.

"Not on my shift," she said cheerfully. "How would I ever earn my free toaster?"

Sitting Twenty-Two

I thought about it all day.

I requested no visitors.

My family was pretty upset with me. They would survive.

Grouch of God had left his Marx on me. See? I can do rim shot jabs, too.

I still didn't understand his last comment. What was up to me? Seemed to me like the words of some well-worn, overly rehearsed motivational speaker.

People are always saying, "It's up to you." But is it? Is it ever up to us? After nature clocks in with the morning weather report, and the house breathes its laments for repair, and the children whine their particular needs, and the car kerplunks and kerplops its aggravations, and the bank account gasps for greater input, and friends and family collide into our space with all of their woes—what part of the day really ends up being "up to us?"

It's all ridiculous.

I prefer dying. Death is the best explanation for life. Here, on the great circular lily pad, I was just another frog—Jonathan Richard Cring, sometime composer, sometime author, sometime musician, sometime husband, sometime father, sometime lover, sometime . . . well, just sometime.

I had a wonderful pity party in progress. All I lacked were refreshments.

"It's up to you."

God, those words bug me. I don't even know if I want it to be up to me. I liked it better when I believed God was preparing a place for me. I liked it better when it was up to God. Isn't He the guy who should have the pressure?

But I don't see Him doing the job, and I know it's not because He's lazy or uncaring. There has to be another reason.

"God, are you preparing a place for me? And if you are, what am I supposed to do until I get there? Because now I know how absolutely magnificent and freeing it is to be spiritual. How can I go back to being, just, well, just me?"

I thought for a long time.

And then I heard—honest to God, I heard—honest to eternity, I heard—the voice of Calm speak to my soul. It was so wonderful to hear him.

Calm said, "Prepare a place for yourself."

I was so happy to hear his familiar voice that I failed to ask him what he meant.

Prepare a place for myself?

How do I do that?

Isn't that presumptuous?

Isn't that playing God?

Isn't He the preparer, and I'm the guest?

Yet there must be some reason I experienced all this stuff. I now know that all truth is the gentle merger of emotion and logic; the message of God is always acceptance and forgiveness; we as beings are heart, soul, mind and strength; we are not alone in this universe; that wherever there are creatures, diversity reigns; that we all share the need for blood, water, fire and air; and that the only blessing is to evolve, and the only true sin is to stagnate.

It's a good start to a great finish.

I don't know how much time I have left on this misshaped orb we call Earth.

But I do know this: that if I can take the little bit of what I know and apply it to everyday hassles, blessing will follow. At the end of every labor, there is always a revelation of a great treasure placed in the earth. And, I have only one mission remaining: make the will that I saw in eternity be done here on earth, even as it was done in Spirit World.

So call me crazy, and surely you must. But for now, you'll find me here, doing what I know to do.

Love those sent my way, living through the hassles, enjoying the labor, and preparing a place for myself.

The End

Jonathan Richard Cring

Jonathan Richard Cring is the composer of ten symphonies, the author of seven books, including **I'M . . . the legend of the son of man, Liary, Holy Peace . . .the story of Iz and Pal, Jesonian, Finding the Lily and Digging for Gold.** His thirty-year experience has taken him from the grease paint of theater to a time as an evangelist among the gospel saints. He is the winner of a Billboard Music Award and is the in-house composer for the Sumner County Symphony. He travels the country lecturing as an advocate for the Jesonian movement. He has been married for thirty-four years and is the father of three sons and guardian to three others. He lives in Hendersonville, Tennessee.

Also from the Author

Jesonian
A decision to take spirituality personally.

Stagnancy is the decision to settle for less than we know we need. In every generation there must be a voice reminding us of our true mission, prodding us on to escape mediocrity and stirring the waters to freshen the stream of thinking. Jesonian is a book that poses the questions in the heart of every human who seeks to find some nourishment for his hardening soul – every man, woman and child who yearns for a message with meaning and wants to escape the rigors of religion and find the true spirit in spirituality.

Finding the Lily (to consider)
A journette of the journey.

When I was a kid, they didn't have Big Men's Stores - at least, none my parents told me about. So my mother would buy me the only pants she could find in my size - work pants.

Dickie work pants. For some reason, she would choose the green ones - the color created by smashing a bag of green peas into a frog. And speaking of being smashed, for some reason, she wouldn't buy them my size, I guess because she didn't want to admit how big I was. And so she would purchase them so small that I would have to suck in to button them. That's what you like when you're fat. Tight green clothes. Of course, these pants were so stiff they could stand by themselves, which I have to admit, came in handy when waiting in line at an amusement park.

Digging for Gold [in the rule]

The Golden Rule, Do unto others as you would have them do unto you, loses some of its gleam and luster when merely decoupaged and hung on a wall in a Sunday School class as some sort of insipid platitude, more an aspiration than a lifestyle.

In DIGGING FOR GOLD (in the rule), author Cring examines the intricacies and passion of the original thought and also offers innovative approaches to turning the "Rule" into a reality.

Chocked full of stories, examples and plans of action, DIGGING is a must for the soul who desires to have their spirituality flowing in the mainstream instead of entombed in the sanctuary of religious redundancy.

Holy Peace . . . *the story of Iz and Pal*

Also from Jonathan Richard Cring

In a basket full of oranges, it is always the singular apple that gains our attention. This is a wonderful characteristic of the human soul. So in our day and age, in the midst of clamoring for resolutions based on military might, a breath of fresh air comes in to the atmosphere of pending war. Amir and Jubal – two boys who grew up on different sides of the tracks of a conflict – one Arab, one Jew. They rename themselves Iz and Pal and determine to maintain their friendship amidst the granite – headed thinking of their friendship amidst the granite-headed thinking of their society. Where their journey takes them, the friends they make along the way, the surprising enemies, and the stunning resolution, will keep you riveted to the brief pages of this odyssey into peace.

Jonathan I'M ... *the legend of the son of man*

A novel on the life of Jesus Christ focusing on his humanity, passion, and personality—highlighting struggles with his family, sexuality, abduction by zealots, humor and wit, and interaction with characters bound by tradition, affection, legalism, politics, and religious fanaticism—congealed into a 416 page entertaining and inspirational quick read; non-theological and mind enriching.

Also from Jonathan Richard Cring

Mr. Kringle's Tales . . .
26 stories 'til Christmas

   Twenty-six great Christmas stories for young and old
An advent calendar of stories ranging from the hilarious
"Gunfight at the Okay Chorale" to the spine-chilling "Mr.
Kringle Visits the President", to the futuristic "Daviatha".

Ask for these titles at and all titles from **LWS Books** at:

• Your local bookstore

• WWW.LWSBOOKS.COM

• WWW.AMAZON.COM

Printed in the United States
200001BV00002B/1-198/A

9 780970 436160